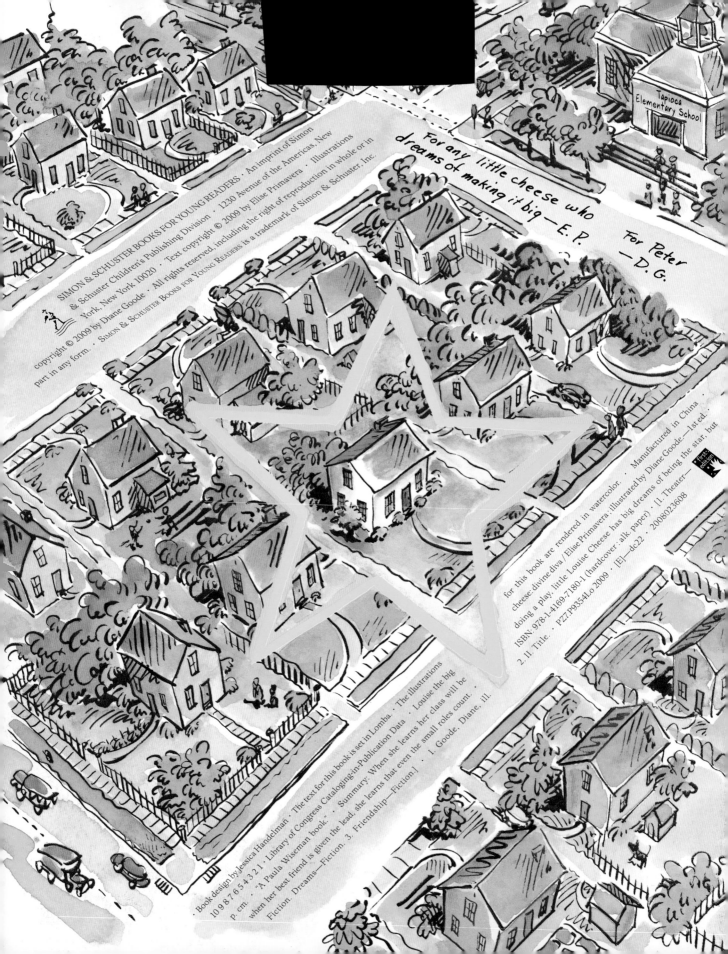

SIMON & SCHUSTER BOOKS FOR YOUNG READERS · An imprint of Simon & Schuster Children's Publishing Division · 1230 Avenue of the Americas, New York, New York 10020 · All rights reserved, including the right of reproduction in whole or in part in any form. · SIMON & SCHUSTER BOOKS FOR YOUNG READERS is a trademark of Simon & Schuster, Inc. · Text copyright © 2009 by Elise Primavera · Illustrations copyright © 2009 by Diane Goode ·

For any little cheese who dreams of making it big — E. P.

For Peter — D. G.

for this book are rendered in watercolor. · Manufactured in China · cheese: divine diva / Elise Primavera ; illustrated by Diane Goode.—1st ed. · doing a play, little Louise Cheese has big dreams of being the star, but ISBN: 978-1-4169-7180-1 (hardcover : alk. paper) · 2009 · [E]—dc22 · 2008023608 2. II. Title. · PZ7.P9354Lo · First edition

Book design by Jessica Handelman · The text for this book is set in Lomba · The illustrations 10 9 8 7 6 5 4 3 2 1 · Library of Congress Cataloging-in-Publication Data · Louise the big p. cm. · "A Paula Wiseman book." · Summary: When she learns her class will be when her best friend is given the lead, she learns that even the small roles count. · I. Goode, Diane, ill. Fiction. Dreams—Fiction. 3. Friendship—Fiction.]

Tapioca Elementary School

LOUISE THE BIG CHEESE

DIVINE DIVA

Elise Primavera

ILLUSTRATED BY Diane Goode

A PAULA WISEMAN BOOK
SIMON & SCHUSTER BOOKS FOR YOUNG READERS
New York London Toronto Sydney

LOUISE CHEESE was a small girl who lived in a sleepy town on a quiet street in a modest house.

She longed for her mother to be the Brownie troop leader. She prayed for her father to be the principal of her school.

But Mr. and Mrs. Cheese did not like the limelight or a lot of fuss.

Louise liked the limelight, she liked a lot of fuss, and more than anything else in the world, she wanted to be a big cheese.

Louise shared a room with her dog, PeeWee. They slept in a tiny bed near a window that looked out to a little crab apple tree that never seemed to get any larger.

She wished she had a room like her big sister, Penelope—with a big mirror where she could look at herself and create hairdos. She wished she had a big bed with a dust ruffle like Penelope's, and a dressing table with tubes of lipsticks with names like Ballet Slipper Pink, Ruby Melt, and Divine Diva.

Because she was so little, Louise was
not allowed in Penelope's room. Ever.

Louise wished she could do her hair like Penelope's. She wished she had Divine Diva lipstick. She wished she could walk right out of her little room, down a red carpet, and become a big star!

"I've heard that it's not so easy to be a big star," Louise's best friend Fern told her when she heard of Louise's plan.

And so at school, when her teacher Mrs. Little announced this year's school play was going to be *Cinderella*, Louise wished she could be Cinderella in the play. This was her chance to be a big star—a divine diva.

She could see herself now—
signing autographs, blowing kisses, being
tossed bouquets of roses. Then maybe there would be a big
director from Broadway in the audience, and he would insist
on her going back with him and being Cinderella there.

Louise's hand shot up because she just knew
she had to be Cinderella in the school play!

"One at a time, girls," Mrs. Little interrupted.

"Girls, girls," Mrs. Little said. "Tomorrow will be tryouts for the part, and then I will decide who will be Cinderella in the school play."

That night after dinner Louise told her mother, her father, Penelope, and PeeWee that she was playing the lead role of Cinderella in the school play and that she would probably be going to Broadway soon.

Her parents said that they would be sad to see her go.

PeeWee cried.

Penelope was glad and said that Louise could even have her tube of Divine Diva lipstick as a going-away present.

The next day at the tryouts Mrs. Little watched Louise dance and she listened to Louise sing.

Mrs. Little watched Fern dance and she listened to Fern sing.

Mrs. Little listened to all the other children sing and dance too.

She had to decide who was going to play the big part of Cinderella, the big part of the prince, the big part of the Fairy Godmother, and the big parts of the evil stepsisters. But not all of the parts were big.

Some roles were small—for instance, the mice.

Louise just knew that she was going to be Cinderella. She felt really sorry for Fern because she was probably going to have to be a mouse.

Very soon Mrs. Little decided.

She decided that Louise would be a mouse
and Fern would be Cinderella.

And Louise meant it.

She did not speak to Fern all that day or the next.

She did not speak to Fern when
the class goldfish died and
they got a guinea pig.

She did not speak to Fern when the girl in the second row got in trouble for coloring her fingernails with red crayon instead of doing a reading assignment. She didn't even speak to Fern when they had a substitute teacher with wrinkly knees.

Now Fern will sign autographs, Louise thought. *Fern will blow kisses and be showered with roses, and Fern will be on Broadway playing Cinderella.*

Things couldn't be worse.

Or could they?

The Monday before the play, they got their costumes.

Fern got a frilly pink big-cheese Cinderella ball gown.

Louise got an itchy gray costume with a tail that kept falling off. The outfit had been one of the three blind mice in the kindergarteners' school play.

At the end of the play Fern got to say, "Fairy Godmother! I have never been so happy in my entire life, and it's all thanks to you!"

Louise got to say, "This way, your Royal Highness," while she held open the door of a cardboard box that was supposed to be a pumpkin carriage.

Fairy Godmother...

By the day of the show Louise felt like she was coming down with something.

Louise went downstairs to tell her parents the truth.

Her mother said, "We would miss you too much if you went to star on Broadway."

Her father said, "It just wouldn't be the same around here."

Just before they left the house, Penelope put some Divine Diva lipstick on Louise's lips.

Finally the curtain was ready to go up. Louise stood in the wings, a little sweaty inside the mouse costume. But wearing the lipstick made Louise decide she didn't look half bad.

The curtain went up. Fern walked onstage and Louise missed her friend already.

The school play went along well. None of the scenery fell down like it kept doing in rehearsal, all the music came right on cue, and Louise's tail managed to stay on.

Louise danced around the cardboard pumpkin carriage, scanning the audience for the important director from Broadway, but all she saw was her family. They waved at her from the third row, and Louise didn't know if it was the Divine Diva lipstick, but she sang and danced better than she ever had before.

Soon it was the grand finale.

Fern raised an arm to deliver her last line and looked more like a big star than Louise ever could have imagined.

"Fairy Godmother!" Fern announced. "Um . . . um . . ."

Louise waited along with the entire audience.

"Fairy Godmother . . . ," Fern said in a little voice, "um, um . . ."

There was complete silence, and Louise could see that Fern's face was white and her hand was trembling.

The audience shifted uncomfortably in their seats and someone coughed.

Fern looked terrified, but could only say, "Um . . . um."

Trying hard not to let anybody see her, Louise whispered out of the side of her mouth to Fern, "I've—never—been— so—happy—in—my—entire—life,—and—it's—all— thanks—to—you."

The audience cheered. The play was over.
The girls took their bows.

As it turned out, there was no big director in the audience or trip to Broadway like Louise had imagined, but she and Fern were friends once more.

When the curtain went down, Fern signed Louise's program and Louise signed Fern's program.

That night Louise went home to her tiny room and climbed into her small bed.

Louise sighed.

The crab apple tree that never seemed to get any larger shimmered in the moonlight, and even though she was still little, somehow Louise couldn't help feeling happy.

I **Still** want to be a **BIG** star on **Broadway**. do you? Take this quiz and see what **your** chances are of becoming a **BIG** CHEESE !!!

Do **you** have what it takes to make it on **BROADWAY**? Choose one for each question and find out!

1. I like to watch:
   a. cartoons and reality shows
   b. old musicals like *Mary Poppins* and *The Wizard of Oz*
   c. baseball games

2. On rainy days I like to:
   a. go to the mall and try on clothes
   b. go to my friend's house and put on a show
   c. go to the TV and put on the baseball game

3. Read this line and memorize it:

Fairy Godmother! I have never been so happy in all my life, and it's **ALL** thanks to you!

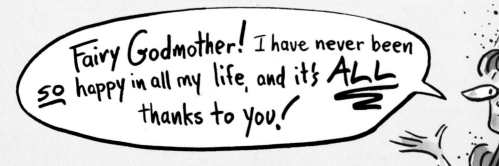

4. If I were a snack, I'd be:

    a. raisins

    b. meatballs

    c. popcorn

5. If I were a song, I'd be:

    a. "Eensy Weensy Spider"

    b. "It's Not Easy Being Green"

    c. "There's No Business
        Like Show Business!"

6. I know:

    a. every single American Girl doll

    b. how to make a peanut butter and jelly sandwich

    c. all the lyrics in *High School Musical*

#7. Please recite the line you memorized a few moments ago from #3.

Answer key: 1. a) medium, b) big, c) little; 2. a) medium, b) big, c) little; 4. a) little, b) medium, c) big; 5. a) little, b) medium, c) big; 6. a) medium, b) little, c) big.